Still
It's ^a Dog's New York

It's ^Still a Dog's New York

A Book of Healing

Susan L. Roth

The following individuals and companies will contribute their proceeds from the sales of this book. With the money raised, the publisher will donate a copy of the book to every elementary school in the New York City and Washington, D.C., metropolitan areas. In addition, funds will go to the ASPCA to help displaced and rescue-worker animals.

Susan L. Roth, author/artist
National Geographic Society, publisher
Quad/Graphics, color separator
Simon & Schuster, distributor

IT'S STILL A DOG'S NEW YORK is a reinterpretation of the artwork used in the author's previous book, IT'S A DOG'S NEW YORK, which took a humorous look at the powerful friendliness of New Yorkers and their pride in their city. After September 11, this same warmth and pride has taken on a new importance, hence the new text and the flags in the hands of the dogs on the cover of IT'S STILL A DOG'S NEW YORK. We hope that readers will enjoy both books, for there is healing power in laughter as well as in comfort.

Thank you to Peter Laufer for the idea; to three dedicated child psychiatrists—Dr. Lenore Terr, Dr. Fredric Solomon, and Dr. Judith Rapoport—for donating their consulting services to make sure that the book speaks as it should to children; and to the staff of National Geographic for putting this project at the top of the list. S.L.R.

This book is dedicated to
America's children—
sad, angry, scared, and, ultimately, hopeful—
in the aftermath of September 11, 2001.

The text is set in Vag Rounded Black, and the display text is set in Cut-Out-Normal,

created by Robert Salazar, based on Susan L. Roth's cut-paper lettering.

Book design by Bea Jackson

Printed in Mexico

ISBN 0-7922-7050-9
Library of Congress Control number: 2001096611

Published by the National Geographic Society.

The world's largest nonprofit scientific and educational organization, the National Geographic Society was founded in 1888 "for the increase and diffusion of geographic knowledge." Since then it has supported scientific exploration and spread information to its more than eight million members worldwide. The National Geographic Society educates and inspires millions every day through magazines, books, television programs, videos, maps and atlases, research grants, the National Geographic Bee, teacher workshops, and innovative classroom materials. The Society is supported through membership dues, charitable donations, and income from the sale of its educational products. Members receive NATIONAL GEOGRAPHIC magazine—the Society's official journal—discounts on Society products and other benefits. For more information about the National Geographic Society, its educational programs and publications, and ways to support its work, please call 1-800-NGS-LINE (647-5463) or write to the following address:

National Geographic Society

1145 17th Street N.W., Washington, D.C. 20036-4688, U.S.A.

Visit the Society's Web site: www.nationalgeographic.com

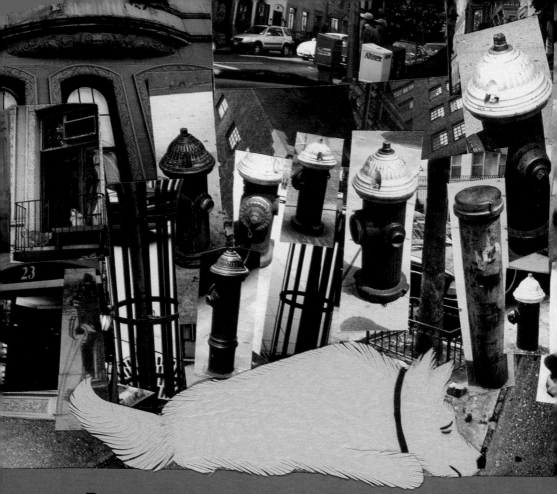

Pepper sat on the sidewalk remembering. He remembered the New York that he loved. It was a beautiful day, but Pepper shut his eyes—until Rover appeared.

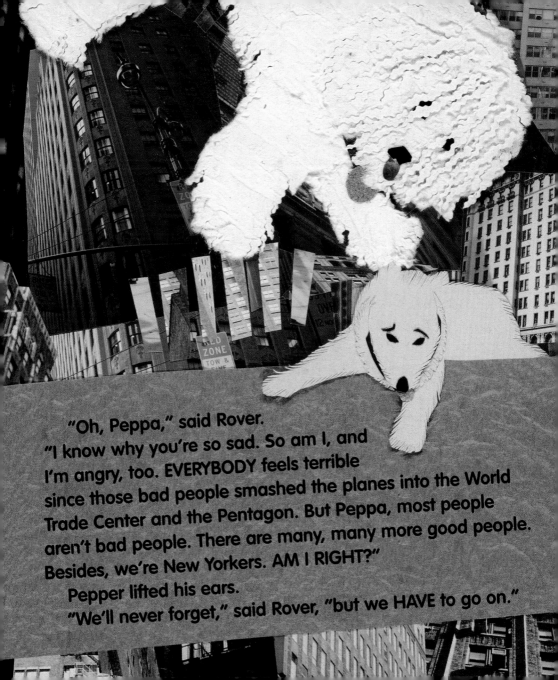

"Oh, Peppa," said Rover. "I know why you're so sad. So am I, and I'm angry, too. EVERYBODY feels terrible since those bad people smashed the planes into the World Trade Center and the Pentagon. But Peppa, most people aren't bad people. There are many, many more good people. Besides, we're New Yorkers. AM I RIGHT?"

Pepper lifted his ears.

"We'll never forget," said Rover, "but we HAVE to go on."

"The World Trade Center towers were taller, but we still have the Empire State Building," said Rover.

"How can you talk about buildings?" said Pepper. "What about the people?"

"I know you feel rotten about them," said Rover. "So do I."

"I can't go to Central Park anymore," said Pepper. "Who wants to run around?"

"If we see sad dogs and cats we could try to cheer them up," said Rover.

"We never talk to cats," said Pepper.

"At a time like this, maybe we should," said Rover.

"I'm still scared to go skating at Rockefeller Center," said Pepper. "What if it happened again there?"

"Don't worry. Big dogs are working twenty-four hours a day to make us safe. You don't have to spend the rest of your life under the bed."

"The pictures are safe at the Metropolitan Museum," said Rover.

"I'd give all those pictures to save somebody's life," said Pepper.

"We didn't get to choose," said Rover. "It's okay to be happy about the pictures."

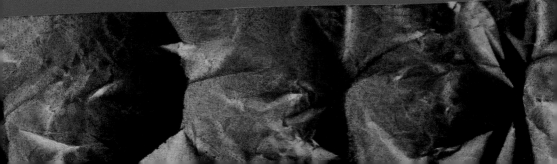

"Carnegie Hall is still here," said Rover.
"Music? Now?" said Pepper.
"Sometimes music makes you feel better," said Rover.

"Maybe if we read all the books and magazines and newspapers in the New York Public Library, we could understand why this happened," said Pepper.

"We could try that," said Rover. "And it would help. And we can roar like the lions against the horrible things that happened. We can roar like lions for peace!"

"We can roar loud enough for the WHOLE WORLD to hear!" said Pepper.

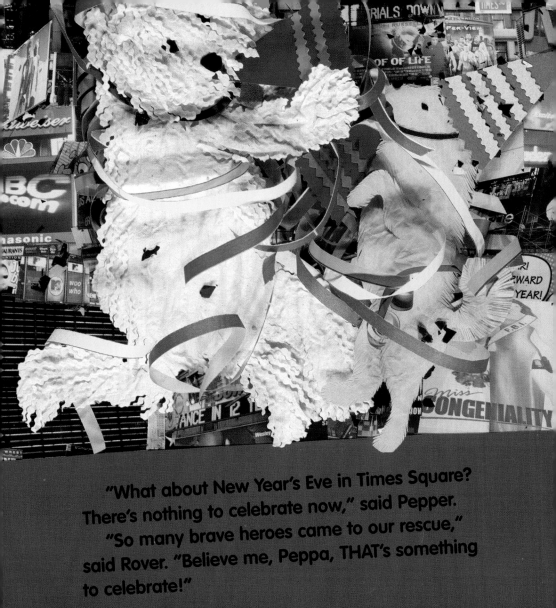

"What about New Year's Eve in Times Square? There's nothing to celebrate now," said Pepper.

"So many brave heroes came to our rescue," said Rover. "Believe me, Peppa, THAT's something to celebrate!"

"A dog could get hungry after all this serious talk," said Rover. "Let's go to Coney Island. Remember, we're still dogs. NOT underdogs, TOP DOGS! Life must go on!"

"That's not easy," said Pepper.

"Who said it would be easy?" said Rover. "We'll have to try very hard, but it's STILL a dog's New York!"

"Look!" said Rover. "The ferryboats are running, just like before. Remember where the World Trade Center was?"

"Those two towers are still in my head," said Pepper, "plain as day!" Remember when you took me up to the top? You could see New Jersey from all the way up there."

"You could see forever," said Rover.

"These are hard times for New York," said Pepper.
"And for all of America," said Rover. "But we're strong."
"We'll get through this if we work hard together."

And they did.

NEW YORK CITY

STATEN ISLAND

Coney Island

BROOKLYN

Staten Island Ferry

Statue of Liberty

World Trade Center

NEW JERSEY

Empire State Building

New York Public Library

Times Square

Rockefeller Center

Carnegie Hall

Metropolitan Museum of Art

Central Park

QUEENS

BRONX

MANHATTAN